CW01506701

Copyright © 2023 Laura Rush

ASIN: B0CDBFVFGY
ISBN: 9798868065231
Imprint: Independently published

Cover design by: Laura Rush

Dedication:

"What is it you want, Mary? What do you want? You want the moon? Just say the word, and I'll throw a lasso around it and pull it down." - George Bailey (Its a wonderful life)

For all the girls waiting on a George Bailey, to sweep you off your feet. Don't lose hope, he will find you soon, when you least expect it.

This ones for you….

May your reading be merry and bright.

So, This is Christmas

by Laura Rush

Chapter 1 – Shaun.

Name me something worse than a cancelled flight due to a small dusting of snow on the runway.

Oh, you can't? No worries, I'll tell you.

Fucking Christmas, that's what!

I should be happy— no, *delighted*— my flight's been cancelled on my way home to New York City. I cannot stand Christmas; the whole thing freaking sucks. Waste of time and money if you ask me. So-called families gather for the 'most wonderful time of year,' the giving of gifts, the decorations, the crazed shoppers, the over-the-top consumption of food… the list is endless.

But even my *bah humbug* ass cannot miss this year. I needed to get home, like, yesterday. My dearest brother decided to drop down on one knee and propose to his darling Kimmy a week ago, and my family thought it would be a grand idea to throw a Christmas Eve celebration party at their house.

I stretch out my legs in front of me, brushing a hand through my hair. My head's pounding with stress; I try cracking my neck from side to side in an attempt to release some tension in it. Turning towards the windows to my left, I watch the snow pick up momentum and fall to the ground.

Looks like I won't be home tonight either. *Fuck!*

Pulling out my iPhone from my pocket, I search for Dad's name and hit the call button. *Here we go... Welcome to hell.*

"Have you arrived yet?" My dad's voice booms down my receiver.

I sigh loudly. "I'm great, Dad, thanks for asking. And no, is the answer to your question. My flight from Paris was cancelled due to snow and it looks like my next flight will be as well." My response is clipped, my annoyance clear.

"Shaun, it's once a year I ask you to be home. You've had three-hundred-and-sixty-five days to plan this. More so, you know how important this year's gathering will be," he snaps back.

Didn't he just hear me? I cannot help, nor predict, the weather forecast!

"I am fully aware of that, Dad, but it's out of my hands!" I say through gritted teeth. My father and I have never seen eye to eye; Mom reckons it's because we' re so alike. How she puts up with his moody ass, I will never know.

"I do not care how you do it, Shaun. Christmas Eve is a few days away, so by hook or crook, you get yourself here and with the best god damn smile on your face when you arrive. I won't have you spoiling it for Jack and Kimberly!" he shouts back at me and hangs up.

I stare at my phone in my hand for a moment, my mouth slack in shock. wondering why the hell he wants me there anyway— the man clearly cannot stand me. Stuffing it back into my pocket and picking up my rucksack off the floor, I walk to find the nearest bar. I need a strong drink to drown my sorry self in.

As I turn to my right, I bump into the mother of all Christmas angels. A petite, chestnut-haired woman looks up at me. She shyly smiles while pushing her glasses back up the bridge of her nose and her bright, ocean- blue eyes bore into mine. I notice how they accentuate the freckles that dot across her nose and rosy cheeks. I step back and my eyes squint now looking at her in full form. I would like to take back my previous comment of 'a Christmas angel' and replace it with a Christmas malfunction. *What the fuck is she wearing?*

A white, light- up 'I heart Xmas' sweater blinds me with twinkling, flashing lights. She's paired it with green leggings and black boots. It takes me a moment to realise that she's speaking to me; I watch her lips move for another second before shaking my head.

"I am sorry, what did you say? Your sweater hindered my eyes so much it temporarily shut down my ability to hear and think," I say, my lips curling in disgust.

She smirks back up at me. "I see. Well, I was saying I'm sorry for bumping into you. But now I am not so sorry. Merry almost-Christmas Eve to you, good Sir." She singsongs the last part out and walks away.

Merry almost-Christmas Eve?

God, if you can hear me, just zap a lightning bolt straight through my head, please.

"Good evening, passengers. This is the pre-boarding announcement for flight 89B to New York City. We are now inviting those passengers with small children, and any passengers requiring special assistance, to begin boarding at this time. Please have your boarding pass and identification ready. Regular boarding will begin in approximately ten minutes' time. Thank you."

Downing the last of my scotch, I stand, a little too wobbly for my liking. Instantly worrying about the fact, I might be too drunk to get on the plane, I signal the bartender to grab me a bottle of water, paying on my card, before heading towards the terminal.

Patience has never been my thing. Even less so when I have had a drink. I push past some happy families hugging loved one's goodbye for the holidays, and march towards where I need to be, cursing and flipping the bird to unhappy people who get in my way. Feeling relieved this hell I have been thrown into is nearing its end, I stand in the queue to get onto the plane. Pulling out my phone, I text Jack— my younger brother, and the favourite child— to tell him that I'm about to catch my flight to New York. I hear a voice pipe up behind me and I let out an audible groan.

"Oh, look who it is; it's Mr Grinch himself!" I can practically hear the smile stretching across her jolly face.

Chapter 2 – Brim

I cover my smile with the book I have in my hand as Grinchy whirls around in my direction. Listen, I am all about bringing the Christmas spirit to all who need it, and Mr Grinch needs it desperately.

It is the season for giving, after all.

He doesn't look like the green haired Grinch I know and love— in-fact, he looks the complete opposite, like he literally walked out of a Vogue magazine shoot. His broad shoulders flex underneath his tight t-shirt as he clenches and unclenches his fists. That beautiful face should be off- putting considering the scowl it wears right now, but it's not. Thick eyebrows that are drawn together nearly cover his long, dark eyelashes and deep brown eyes. He has a perfect shaped nose and kissable lips, with the final addition of a strong shaped jaw line. *He's like fucking Hercules.*

I snap out of my perving, removing my bottom lip

from my teeth and ask him, "What were you saying? Sorry."

"I see you're still wearing that offensive sweater," he says in a dry voice, while putting on a pair of sunglasses.

"What's with the glasses?" I ask, immediately regretting it, knowing his next response will be something to insult my lovely, hand- knitted jumper.

Raising a brow at me, he sighs heavily. "Isn't it obvious, Fruit Loop?" He stretches out his free hand to flick a light on my jumper. *True Grinch style.*

I bite my bottom lip again to cover my incoming smile.

"That's the second time you've complimented my sweater. You want one, too?" I say while not looking at him and pulling my bag in front of me to pretend I' m looking for something. I' m not, but he's so fun to mess with. "I'm sure I have a matching one in my bag; you can totally have it if you want!"

"Urh, God, it's me again. Listen, about that lightning bolt I asked you for earlier; if you could just do it already, that would be grand," he mutters under his breath. I glance up to see him staring up at the ceiling, eyes closed and hands in the prayer position in front of his chest. I hide another laugh with my hand.

A lady's voice interrupts my next comeback. "Excuse me, sir, ma'am— can I see your boarding passes?" I look over Grinchy's shoulder to see a slender air hostess looking at us both.

"Oh, thank God! That's a better idea," he grumbles, and turns to hand his ticket to the lady.

"And your wife's ticket, sir?" she points at me. I laugh aloud and grab Grinchy's arm before he can respond to her.

"Excuse my husband. H e's very tired and we are both eager to get home to our children, Joseph, and Joy," I say, smiling sweetly at her. I hand my boarding pass over while Mr Grinch gapes at me, opened- mouthed. She wishes us both a Merry Christmas and hopes we will be reunited with our children soon. I pull at his arm, ignoring the tingles I feel from touching him, and drag him towards the plane.

Snapping out of his trance, he halts us both on the spot before shouting, "You're a fucking crazy woman!" I laugh in response.

In my best baby-talk voice, I say, "Nooow, where's that Christmaaas spirit gooone? Heeey hubby, you don't want our children to see you all grumpy this year, do you?"

"Just stay away from me, Fruit Loop, okay?" H is brows furrow as he frostily points his finger at my

9

nose. I pretend to bite it a nd his eyes widen before he turns on his heel and stomps down the tunnel.

My smile stretches across my face, and I turn to follow him onto the plane.

I read Seat 68B on my ticket before handing it over to an air hostess and stuffing my book into my bag. She says something while I glance around to try and find my seat. Too embarrassed about not paying attention to her to ask her what she said, I head towards the economy section. Hopefully, my seat neighbour will let me have the window seat instead. With it being a nine-**hour** flight, I need to be able to look out the window, even if it is pitch black outside.

Finally finding my seat, I turn towards the grumpy face looking up at me from his seat next to the window and break out into a smile while my insides melt.

Placing a hand to my chest, I stare into his hateful eyes and wink. "Jingle my bells, this is a Christmas miracle!"

Chapter 3 – Shaun.

I am being punished. God is breaking me for making too many requests.

That is, it, I am getting off this plane! There is no way in hell that I am spending the next nine hours sat next to fucking Cindy Lou Who herself. I stand up abruptly, snatching my bag off the ground.

"Get out of my way, Fruit Loop. I am getting off," I **snap** at her. Staring into her eyes, I hope my anger radiates through her body and the lights on her sweater catch flames, burning it to the ground in front of me. *Now, that would be a Christmas miracle.*

The air hostess comes into view from behind Fruit Loop and asks if there is a problem. She tells me I need to sit down and buckle up because we' re ready for take-off. Fruit Loop doesn't take her eyes off me the entire time.

"Yeah, there's a problem— either find me another seat or I'm getting off this fucking plane!" I erupt at her. I know I' m being a dick but that has been my go-to armour my whole life, so why stop now, right?

The air hostess gasps loudly at my tone before fixing her face into a stern look. "Sir, I will not tolerate you speaking to me like that. There are no other seats and unfortunately, we are about to take off. So, I'm going to ask you again, please take your seat and put your belt on before I call in security."

The captain's announcement comes over the speakers of the plane, informing us all we are about to take off, and I huff my annoyance to them both before sitting down in my seat again and stuffing my bag under my chair.

Fruit Loop must notice my empty level of Christmas spirit and chooses not to look or speak to me again for the next hour.

Chapter 4 – Brim

'So, this is Christmas
And what have you done?
Another year over
And a new one just begun

And so this is Christmas
I hope you have fun
The near and the dear one
The old and the young.'

I am mid-way listening to the all-time greatest ever Christmas song when my headphones are viciously ripped from my ears.

"Please, I'm begging you to stop. *Please.*"

I scowl over at Grinchy who's holding one end of my earphones in his hand.

"Give me that back, you scrooge." I lean across him to get the other earphone out of his vice grip.

"No. You've been singing the same song on repeat for

the last thirty minutes and I can't take much more of it." His eyes plead with me to stop, and I grin back at him. "So, what can I sing then?"

He tilts his head to the side and dryly replies, "Nothing."

Raising my brow and throwing him a questioning gaze. "Well, what do you propose we do instead?"

Shuffling his butt further away towards the window, he side- eyes me in horror, shaking his head. "We? There is no *we,* Fruit Loop." He pauses when his arm hits the window and he glances towards it, sighing loudly because he can't put more distance between us. He continues, "You can't sing, and I need sleep, so if you could be a doll and be quiet for a while, THAT would suit me perfectly."

I throw my head back laughing, then roll my eyes dramatically at him. "That's boooooring," I drag out.

"Do not care," he grumbles under his breath, then closes his eyes.

Leaning towards him, I whisper, "Psst." He ignores me, of course, so I psst" again, this time poking him in his shoulder. Again, he ignores me.

Throwing my hands up in the air, I sigh in defeat. "Okay, fine, you win. But just for the record," I pause when he opens one eye at me, "I *can* sing. Not perfectly, but I can."

Huffing at me, he turns in my direction to face me. "My ears are still bleeding, and my eyes... can't you turn off those flashing lights on your sweater?" He points a finger at the green twinkling light on my breast.

I giggle. "No, I cannot," I say whilst crossing my arms over my chest.

Grumbling some more incoherent words at me, I hear him say something along the lines of *'Stupid Christmas, stupid sweater.'*

"Well, Fruit Loop, apparently you and that hideous jumper will not let me sleep. You can't keep your mouth shut, so what do you propose we do instead?" A hint of teasing comes from his last words, and I feel the need to squeeze my legs shut. I lick my lips as I stare at his plump ones.

"Urh, well–" I'm about to answer his question when a head pops up between the gap of our seats. A woman with blonde hair, styled in a pixie cut, grins at me widely before turning her head towards Mr Grinch.

"Don't mind me, but you could exchange names." She beams at us, her tone excited, like she's enjoying the mounting tension between him and me.

I nod slowly at her before turning to him, holding out my hand for him to shake. "Brimley Sadie Harris, but everyone calls me Brim."

He grumbles, *this is nonsense,* before reluctantly taking my hand in his and announcing his name. "Shaun Dawson." His eyes hold mine while the rest of his face is expressionless. My mind begins to wonder why he hasn't let go of my hand yet, although it doesn't feel uncomfortable, It's oddly comforting.

The pixie cut girl speaks up again, breaking our trance." The exchanging of names has just begun; soon the mating dance will commence. Though lucky enough to travel to many places in my life and have seen many wonders, this could just well be the greatest one of all." Her voice is full of excitement, as she holds up her Dictaphone close to her mouth.

Shaun leans forward and taps her shoulder, causing her to stop and press the pause button on the side. "What are you doing?" His words come out clipped while his nostril s flare.

"I'm making a documentary." She shrugs her shoulders and looks at us like we should have known that's what she's doing.

His hand grips mine tighter as he shouts, "Oh, for fuck's sake!" It causes all the passengers to turn and look at us. Unsure what to do in this exact moment, I just rub my thumb softly over the top of his hand. You know, to comfort him in his hour of need, not because I am desperate to hold his hand longer or anything like that. It's what the Baby Jesus would have wanted, right?

Shaun's lips pinch together as a pained look crosses his face. Scratching the back of his neck, he mumbles, "This is just perfect; I'm stuck on a goddamn plane for the next eight hours with a David Attenborough wanna-be and Mrs Claus."

Squeezing his hand, his head whips over in my direction, like he's just put two and two together and realised we are still holding hands.

"It's okay. Shaun. M y lights can turn off and I'm sure–" I nod my head to our narrator's direction in front of us and mouth silently, "–will get bored soon." I reluctantly let go of his hand to flip the bottom of my jumper over and press the button, turning the lights off.

Softening his features, he gives me his first real smile. "Thanks. Uh, I'm sorry. It's been a difficult day, that's all."

Chapter 5 – Shaun.

It always takes so long to calm down my nerves when I'm irate. I feel them swirling around inside my stomach, and I can't seem to get my hands to stop trembling. Dragging my sweaty palms up and down my trousers, I take a few deep breaths. In and out. In and out.

It's not working though, so I lean over and grab Brim's free hand. A small gasp leaves her, but she quickly gets back to rubbing her thumb over the top of my hand like before, without uttering a word to me. I know it's strange, right? To hold a stranger's hand on a plane, especially since you haven't been that welcoming and kind to them. But her calm, quiet presence right now is the only thing stopping me from running to the back of the plane and opening the door, before jumping to certain death.

I hate this time of year. The thought of facing my father and living under the same roof as him again, even for just a few days, pushes me to breaking point. I just don't understand why he can't treat me like Jack.

"What do you do for work?" Brim's soft voice pulls me out of my thoughts, and she turns to face me straight on, lifting her legs up to sit cross legged. Giving me a small smile while gently rubbing my hands with hers as if they are cold, she waits patiently for me to answer her.

"I'm a wine maker." I watch her eyes widen and her mouth opens and closes trying to get words out. I continue, "I'm in charge of the entire wine making process— sources, production, bottling, and selling. I own The Merlot Man in Manhattan."

I've always loved my work ever since I was a young boy. I had this fascination with what adults w ere drinking that I couldn't. My dad was the mayor of New York. Grand parties, galas, and public events around the city w ere a weekly thing for me. I had to sit in the corner and watch as he moved around the room, talking to every person. Pretending I wasn't there, I had to blend into the walls and be seen but not heard. Every person in any room I was in had a glass filled to the top with this strong-smelling liquid.

So, naturally, my curiosity peaked, and I remember the first time I tried some wine. The harsh, rich body trickled down my throat as the fruity after taste lingered on my tongue. I hated it. But each week, each event, I'd sip an assorted colour or smelling wine. By the time I had gotten to my teenage years,

I'd tried most wines I could get my hands on. I would find myself researching unusual ways to make it and coming up with new flavours to make wine better.

Throwing her hands in the air, Brim beams at me. "That's *so* fucking cool!" She pops every word and I grin widely back at her. I huff a laugh and give my thanks. "What do you do, Fruit Loop?"

"Well, it's not as good as your job, but I'm a professional matchmaker." Now it's my turn to look at her wildly. She giggles and pulls at the bottom of her sweater. "My sisters and I started an online dating site where we set people up based on their preferences, interests, stars signs, aspirations in life." She waves her hand in front of her face. "Based on anything, really."

"Wow" I nod my head in surprise. Who'd have thought the Christmas tree hugger was a match maker?

She bites her lower lip and furrows her brows. "You seem speechless," she comments quietly.

I nod. "Yeah, I kind of am, I guess. I just figured you were a cookie maker or Santa's little helper." She barks out a laugh, bringing music to my ears.

"You said sisters; how many do you have?"

She nods, looking down at her sweater again. "I have five sisters. No brothers— it was a house full of girls at one point for dad."

Shit, mommy and daddy didn't own a tv by the sounds of it. "Five sisters? Jesus, that's a lot. I only have one younger brother, Jack. My parents were hoping for one of each. I'd have loved a little sister, I think."

Brim's about to reply to me when our narrator pipes up again. "So, the courtship display has finally begun. The male opens up, showing the female he does have a heart, after all. Maybe he can attract this strong female."

Brim slaps her hand over her face and her cheeks turn pink. I mouth it's okay silently to her and rub my thumb over the back of her hand like she did for me.

We chat a little while longer, sipping our wine handed to us by the air hostess, and I must admit, it has been a while since I've had a normal conversation with a woman. Well, anyone for that matter. I explain the process of tasting wine to her, and she tells me all about her sisters: Rory, Annie, Francesca, Abbey, and Lottie. I get the feeling though halfway through our chat Brim wasn't good with alcohol and might be tipsy off one glass.

"Let's play a game," she says, while flopping into the side of me. She looks up at my face and her eyes are glossy, while her pupils are dilated.

I smile down at her. "Shouldn't you try sleeping?" Pouting at me, she points a finger in my direction. "No, I wanna play a game." I laugh at her child-like response and answer her in quick defeat. "Okay, Fruit Loop, what's the game?"

"Puns! Christmas puns— the aim of the game is to fit in as many Christmas puns as possible for the rest of the flight. The one with the most at the end is the winner, simple."

"That's stupid, and no to Christmas," I answer, shuffling uncomfortably in my seat.

Arguing back, she angrily asks, "What's your deal with Christmas anyway? It's the most wonderful time of year."

"For some, yeah, it might be but for others it isn't, okay, Brimley?" M y sharp tone was completely unwarranted, I know that, but I can't help it. The cheery disposition and naivety sets me on edge.

"Frosty the snowman's personal affairs are snow-body's business," the lady with the Dictaphone calls out. Brim starts uncontrollably laughing, setting me off too. Brim calls back, "Icy what you did there," gaining a few more laughs from other passengers seated nearby.

I stop laughing and turn my face serious. "It's snow joke, Fruit Loop." I wink at her for good measure.

"Ahhhhhh! He came, he thawed, he conquered," comes from behind me. I turn to see an old couple grinning at Brim and me, and I shake my head back and forth. You know the saying, *if you can' t beat them, join them.*

"Yeah, well, I'm holding on for deer life here," I grumble back and glance at Brim. She's eyeing me curiously and nibbling the inside of her cheek. Without thinking, I lean across the seat and rub her jaw line, feeling tingles rush through my fingers. I quickly pull my hand away and remind myself I don't know her. I'm still unsure why I'm so comfortable around her.

Leaning back into my seat, I close my eyes, listening to the narrator, the old man behind me, and Brim as they drop some more puns, before darkness takes over and I drift off to sleep.

Chapter 6 – Brim.

It's about six hours into our flight when the captain comes over the speaker and announces that there's too much snow to land in New York, and we are now being redirected to Boston. Utter chaos surges through the plane as people begin shouting curse words and questioning the staff on board. The air hostesses are fleeting up and down the aisles, answering questions from concerned passengers. I try to catch one lady, but she hurries down to calm a young couple with a baby. Panic starts rising as I remember I used the last of my cash I had brought with me to Paris on this flight. What the hell am I going to do?

"Relax, Brim," Shaun pipes up from beside me. I turn to look at him; his face is calm and collected — in fact, this is the most relaxed he's looked since I bumped into him at the airport. Feeling tears prick my eyes when he gives me a strong decisive nod with unwavering eye contact, his soft tone reaches out to me. "It's not that bad. They will get us on the next flight from Boston to New York come morning."

I nod back, wringing my hands in front of me. *Let's hope so.*

We land in Boston around two a.m. I follow the crowd through security and hand the clerk on the desk my passport. I've always disliked this part— I feel like I'm in trouble for something, but I don't know what that trouble is. The gentleman at the desk glances at my passport, then up at me, and then back to my passport, before handing it back over and nodding towards the crowd. I furrow my brows at him before I head to collect my baggage. I see Shaun standing by the conveyor belt, waiting for his bag to come through. He's puffing out his cheeks and staring up at the ceiling. Unsure if I should head over towards him, I find my feet are moving me in his direction anyway.

Standing on my tiptoes, I tap him on the shoulder. "Are you okay?" I ask shakily.

Looking down at me, he slowly releases a deep breath before replying in almost a whisper, "Yeah, Fruit Loop, I'm fine. Just–" He gesture s around the airport with his hands. "Manic, you know? Too many people for me."

I nod in response as parts of him slowly click into place in my mind. His need for quiet time and peace. I'm guessing as a wine maker, he must work solo for some periods, which I'm betting is his favourite time to be in work.

"I get it. Is there any word on what's happening?" I rub his arm up and down; his features soften, and he shakes his head. I overhear a guy behind us with a strong southern accent answering my question.

"There aren't any flights in or out, we were the last ones in. They are putting on coaches, or there's a train heading down south, but for how long before it gets stuck in snow, I don't know."

The lady he's talking to shrieks loudly. My chest tightens at the man's words. My heart beats rapidly in my chest and I place a hand over my heart, feeling the quickened thumping as my breathing accelerates.

Frantically darting my gaze around—I must look like a crazy woman— I choose not to wait to hear any more of what he has to say. Spotting my suitcase coming round the conveyor belt, I run to grab it quickly and rush out toward the boards to check for myself.

Shit, shit, shit. **CANCELLED** *is listed* next to every flight in or out on all of the boards. *Shit.*

Beads of sweat form on my face and I feel my cheeks

reddening. I pull my phone from my bag and dial my sister Francesca's number.

"Franny, I'm stuck— like, really stuck. Stranded, some would say," I rush out before she has a chance to say hello. I relay the entire details, including the no money, to her before catching my breath.

"Well, shit, Brim!" I hear her rushing down the stairs to my dad and mom, telling them what I'd just offloaded onto her.

"Brimley, kid, you there?" My dad's concerned voice comes through, and I crack, sitting down on the closest chair and sobbing to him. I'd hate to miss Christmas with my family. It's the one time of year we all shut down our devices in the house and turn back the clock to the old days, playing board games, watching Christmas films, eating endless amounts of buffets Mom makes, and watching dad lose it at charades.

"Hey, it's okay. Your moms just wired you some money over; it should be in your account now. See about the coach or train and if you get really stuck, I can come get you. Or if you want, I can come get you now. I think I can get to you in about four, five hours, give or take some time for the snow." I feel my chest clench and my heart break that my dad would do that for me. But I can't let him.

"No, Dad. I f you get stuck, then what will we do? I'll find a way home, I promise." I try to even out my voice to relax him. I hear Shaun shouting from behind me and I pull my phone away from my ear and turn to look at him. He's pacing back and forth in front of the boards, cursing whoever he is on the phone to. "Dad, I've got to go. I'll call you soon, okay? I just noticed I'm on 45% battery. I need to save it in case I need it. T ell Mom I said thank you. I love you all." I hurry to get my words out and hang up. I feel bad for off-loading on them and then taking money, but I do need to save my phone battery.

I look back over at Shaun, and he shouts, "Fuck you!" as he's stuffing his phone back into his jeans pocket. He looks up and we lock eyes for a beat. He mutters something before shaking his head and storming off towards the exit.

Rude.

I manage to take my seat on the train, breathing a heavy sigh of relief. After a crammed shuttle bus ride to the train station, I 'm thankful I am at least in America and not still in Paris with no way of getting home. Taking the train instead of the coach, figuring if I rode the train and it did get stuck in the snow, at least I'll be closer to home, with it being a faster mode of transportation than a bus getting stuck with a load of already unhappy people on.

"Happy Christmas Eve's Eve to me," I whisper as I lift a bottle of water out of my bag. *Just keep thinking happy thoughts. Christmas trees; Christmas pudding; Christmas presents; Mom and Dad in matching Christmas jumpers.* Already feeling better, I continue telling myself I am going to make it home in time.

Chapter 7 – Shaun.

It's a little past four a.m. when I finally take my seat on the train.

I had argued a few more times with my father—I already knew how he'd react, and it didn't help the freaking signal kept cutting out and the line kept going dead on him, which was making him angrier each time he had to call back. I didn't answer a few times just to calm my nerves so when I did, he was shouting about how I'm a disgrace; that I need to be home before the party starts and not a minute later. A nd the last phone call, which nearly made me miss the shuttle ride to the train station, he told me that I must be doing this on purpose. *Yeah, sure thing, Dad.*

It's Christmas— dare I say it— Eve's Eve . So, I've got twenty-four hours to get back for the party. *Ugh, I can't think of anything worse right now.*

When the announcement came from the captain that the plane was being redirected, a sense of calm washed over me. The longer I take to get to my parents' place, the less time I have to spend with them. But in turn, the headache over being late is worse.

I look out the window as the train speeds down the tracks. Although it's nighttime, you can still make out the silhouette of trees quickly passing us by. The sky above is slowly turning from black to orange and red as sunset washes over the darkness.

Glancing away from the window, I can't help myself to see if I can spot Brim sitting down somewhere in the carriage. Not that I care really... though a part of me ached when I took in her tear-streaked face sitting in the airport. I had a moment where I thought I would go over to see if she was okay, however I changed my mind when I saw her sweater blinking multi coloured lights and an all too well reminder of what's coming for me tomorrow changed that idea.

I am sure she's fine.

I wake suddenly as my body is jerked forward and back. It takes a second for me to remember I'm on a train, and I rub my hand down my face. A screech comes from the tracks and the train shunts forward and back again. I look around and then out the window; trees either side of the train, all covered in a thick coating of snow. It looks beautiful. Lord only knows where we are, but it's definitely not New York. Flicking my wrist to check the time on my watch, I see it's past seven thirty a.m. which makes me mutter *you've got to be kidding me* under my breath. I stretch my arms above my head, letting out a long yawn.

"Hey, do you know what's going on, man?" I ask a teenage kid that's just walked past me.

He looks at me with his mouth open and throws me a flat gaze before replying, "Yeah, we've stopped." No *shit Sherlock, I can see that*, is what I want to reply but instead I just wave him off and pick up my things, following the direction to where he was heading.

Joining the line of passengers, making their way off the train, I spot Brim up ahead. Although I can't see her face, I know it's her. Her long brown hair is wrapped up in a bun on the top of her head, and her signature bright green leggings make her easy to spot.

Passing the conductor by the doors, I ask him where we are. "Not far from the Willington Rest Area. I-84 eastbound in Connecticut, sir."

I shake my head in disbelief and rub the back of my neck, still not completely awake from the last twenty-four hours. "Incoming, err, stupid question but–" I pause to sheepishly look at him, and he gets where I'm going with it.

"Snow is too much on the track to move forward and it's gonna be hours, if not overnight, before they can get the tracks clear. You'll have to head towards the rest area and see what's available up there for the time being. We will get word to you all when you can board again."

Accepting defeat and a nod of thanks I step off the train. *I'm officially, if not already, on Dad's shit list.*

Spotting Brim again, struggling to pull her flower-covered suitcase alongside the tracks as the snow falls heavily down. I pull my jacket tighter around my body, deciding to go help her out. *You never know, Santa might still come and rescue me if I do.* Yeah, who am I kidding?

Coming up behind her, I throw my rucksack on my back and move my holdall into one hand, then grabbing the handle of her suitcase with my free hand, I take it off her. She shrieks loudly and moves her hands to her chest, breathing heavily in and out.

"You good?" I ask, not looking at her but following the rest of the people who were on the train up ahead. She sighs loudly, then replies in a shaky voice, "Not really."

Nodding my head in agreement. "Yeah," I huff out, "me too."

She sniffles a few times before I look down and see her pulling at her white sweater sleeve and using it to wipe the tears streaming down her face. Stopping us both, I turn to her. "Hey, look at me, Fruit Loop," I soothe as I wait for her to meet my eyes, placing my hands on her shoulders. I tell her, "The rest stop's a little way up here. Once you've had some food and sleep, you'll feel much better. You are going to get home, okay?" I try to reassure her.

More tears flow down her cheeks and I swipe them away with my thumbs, before letting her go to pick up my bag and pull her suitcase behind me.

"Why are you helping me?" Brim questions from behind me.

Choosing to ignore her because frankly, I don't have that answer, I reply back with something I know will make her smile too. "Come on, Mary, I'm taking you to Nazareth." A huge smile breaks out on my face as I say it and I hear her giggle.

"Are you the donkey?" Stopping again, I whirl around to face her, pinching the bridge of my nose. I take a few collected breaths before shaking my head. "What? No, I'm not. I am Joseph, of course."

"You look like you could be the donkey, though," she says, winking at me .

Throwing my hands up in the air, I raise a brow at her, waiting for an explanation as to why I am the donkey. *I'm guessing it's because I 'am rideable,* wink, wink.

"Paaah!" she barks out, holding her stomach while laughing. "Your. Face. Ooooh, what a picture!"

I purse my lips to stop myself smiling and turn my back to her, resuming my hike to the rest area.

"I'm sorry, Sir. There is only one room available," the lady behind the motel desk replies, not looking up at me while flipping through a magazine in front of her.

"Only. One. Room?" I punctuate every word through gritted teeth.

She finally looks up from the pages and raises a brow at me, while chewing on gum like she's some sort of fucking cow eating grass. "Mm, that's what I said, honey," she sarcastically drags out. She pretends to search on the computer in front of her, tapping on the keyboard with her ridiculously blinged up, neon-coloured, fake nails on, *mmh*'ing and tutting as she stares at the screen. Placing both my hands on the countertop, I wait for her to speak, hopeful she might find two rooms. "So, you want that room or not, darling?"

Sucking in a long deep breath through my nose, I give her my best hateful glare I can muster. "I suppose I will have to." I rummage through my pockets and pull out my wallet, muttering *it better be the fucking honeymoon suite, honey,* before I throw cash at her. She smirks and flicks through the money, then stands up from the chair. Her heels click along the wooden floor before coming to a stop at the key safe. Throwing her head over her shoulder, she winks. "It's the best room we have."

Chapter 8 – Brim.

Losing Shaun, a couple of hours ago. He kindly helped me with my suitcase along the tracks and up towards the rest area. His phone started blowing up with calls— from who, I don't know— and he stepped away from me to go answer them.

The train, unfortunately for me, isn't going to be running tonight. We had the conductor turn up earlier and promise they should be able to get everyone boarded tomorrow morning. He said they are still clearing the tracks but by the time they've cleared one part and moved onto the next, the snow has already fallen on the track they just cleared. The weather forecast is meant to be a clear night tonight, so with no more snow fall, I should make it back home by the afternoon. *Fingers and toes crossed, right?*

I walk into the Saltwood motel to get myself a room for the night. Shaun was right: a bit of food and sleep will do me good. I stand at the desk and notice a bell on top of the counter. Pressing it down once, it rings. A few moments later, a bleached- blonde haired lady steps out from the room behind the desk. Before I get a chance to open my mouth, she beats me to it.

"There ain't no more rooms, honey." *Okaaaaay, that's great news.*

She looks me up and down with her hand crossed over her chest, head tilting to the side, while chewing gum like a fucking cow. "There's a couch over there," she points to a place behind me. "It will cost you, though." She gestures at the *pay me* sign with her hands. I curl my lips in disgust, and she raises a brow, smirking.

"She isn't sleeping on that chlamydia- ridden thing," Shaun's voice booms from the front door. I turn to face him and see that his hairs' still wet from the shower he's clearly just had, and he's dressed in grey sweatpants and a white t-shirt, with a black puffer jacket over the top. I turn back towards the lady who just laughs loudly at us. "Suit yourself." She waves him off and goes back into the room behind the desk.

"Brim," his soft voice calls out to me. "Come on." He takes my suitcase out of my hand and turns towards the front door. Taken back by him showing up, I open my mouth to ask him where he's taking me, then close it again, a weird feeling crossing over me. I should be terrified at this moment, but I'm not.

Why does he make me feel safe?

Like he can read my thoughts, he says, "I booked the last room. I tried to get you one too, but–" He turns to me and shrugs. *He tried to get me a room. Why?* His cheeks turn a deep red colour, and he looks away, rubbing the back of his neck with his free hand. "You can bunk in my room for the night, if you want." He shakes his head and looks dead ahead, while guiding me across the parking lot and towards the row of rooms behind it.

"Thank you," are the only words I can get out. Abbey, one of my sisters, would be shocked at me with my speechless ways right now. If I told her, she wouldn't believe me— Abbey always complains I talk too much.

He stops in front of door number eight, putting the key in and turning the lock. "Welcome home, Fruit Loop," he says, and steps to one side to let me go before him.

"Thank you," I say again, before stepping inside and stopping in the middle of the room. I look around the small area, noticing a bathroom off to one side of the room. Ill- fitted carpets line the floor, cut, and burnt in places. The smell in the room stinks of liquor and stale cigarettes. I spot a random wicker chair in the corner of the room, and then a dead Christmas tree next to it. The lights that were once on the tree are now on the floor with the Pine-needles and I laugh. "At least they decorated for the holidays," I say through giggles.

Shaun laughs behind me. "I don't think that was decorated this year, *or* last year," he replies, and I turn to face him. I notice only one double bed that he's sat on right now, with two bedside tables on either side. His belongings lay on the floor beside his side of the bed, and my suitcase sits on the other side. My cheeks light up as the sudden realisation hits me like a freight train...

There is only one bed... Why didn't I think of this before?

"Err, Grinchy..." I pause, pointing at the bed then looking around the room, hoping there's a settee somewhere or a camp bed. Something I could sleep on. "Yeah, Fruit Loop?" his voice sounds sultry and a little bit amused at the same time, ringing through my ears.

"There's only one bed," I shakily say aloud.

"Yeah, looks that way, honey," he mocks. I glance up at him through my lashes and his face is split with a shit- eating grin plastered on.

"So?" I say, while bouncing up and down on the balls of my feet. He leans forward and places a pillow behind his back, clearly amused with the fact I've just clocked that I will either need to sleep next to him in that bed, or sleep on the dirty, stinky floor.

He picks up his phone and holds it to his mouth like it's a microphone,

"The female deer seems caught in the headlights, appearing stuck in flight or fight mode as she stands in the middle of the motel room. Will she climb into bed with this charming elk and go to sleep, or will she sprint right out the room? Only time will tell." He winks and continues. "Her movements are slow and considered... She looks like she might be heading for the door, though she knows that possible pneumonia comes should she step outside." I smile at his antics, dropping my hunched shoulders and taking one step towards the bed. He smiles and pulls his phone back to the microphone position. "For the female deer, danger awaits," he jokes in a deep voice. I laugh and take a step back.

"Come on, Fruit Loop, I don't bite. It's just a bed, and we both need to rest." He taps the side of the bed that's empty and I feel my whole body rise in heat.

"I need to shower," I say in a whisper voice.

"Soooo, go shower," he counters back, then goes back to playing on his phone.

"Okay, I will," I say, my voice sounding almost normal this time. I grab my things from my suitcase, feeling his eyes on me. Part of me kind of likes it.

Wandering into the bathroom and, shock horror, it's hanging on by a thread. Tiles are cracked, the shower curtain is only looped on a few hooks, and the sink is covered in limescale around the taps. *Eww.*

Undressing and placing my clothes on a hook behind the door, and my towel on the hook near the shower, I turn the shower on at the wall. I adjust the dials until I find the right temperature; it's possibly the only thing that works in this motel room like it should.

Letting the water fall across my body, I crank up the hot tap a little more to feel the stress of the last twenty-four hours melt away. Steam fogs my vision and I stretch down to pick up the shampoo I'd just put in here. I finally find it and pour some in my hands without thinking to actually look at the bottle.

The smell of Shaun's minty Fragrance hits me first as I rub the contents into my hair. *Fuck.* I bend over to pick the bottle back up to confirm my suspicions that I've accidentally used the body wash of the guy who I only met yesterday and am now bunking in the same room with. When the soap runs into my eyes, instantly stinging them, I curse aloud and then fumble around the shower curtain to get my towel, when I slip on the tiles and fall like a sack of potatoes to the floor. *Ouch! Fuck, that hurt.*

Holding the side of my hip as the pain throbs, no doubt leaving a nasty bruise. And then I start to cry.

"Fuck this. Fuck the plane, fuck the train, fuck this hellhole of a motel, fuck that stupid shower and curtain, fuck my eyes… just fuck it all!"

"Fuck your eyes?" I hear come from behind the door questioningly.

"Yes, Mr Grinch, fuck my eyes," I sob, as the water starts to burn my back.

"Okay, well, when you put it like that…" I know he's not being serious; I can hear the tease in his voice, and it makes me smile slightly.

"You, okay?" he asks softly when I don't reply.

"Nooo," I drag out between hiccups. "I accidently used your shower stuff, thinking it was my shampoo, and when it got into my eyes, I slipped and bashed my hip," I sniffle out.

He curses under his breath. "A re you hurt?" The door slightly opens. I can see him, but I cover myself with the now fully broken curtain so he can't see my goods.

Lord knows what I look like, slumped on the floor, with mascara all down my face and shampoo in my hair. I put my head back under the shower to rinse the soap out of my hair, letting it wash away the soap in my eyes at the same time.

"My hip hurts." I try to move to stand up but stop when I wince in pain as it shoots up my side.

"Okay, I'm coming in." Before I can stop him, the door swings open and his hand is covering his eyes. He takes slow steps towards me as he swings his arm about in front of him. He does this for a few seconds until it lands on my clothes, then grabbing from the side and throwing them to me, he tells me, "Use that towel to cover yourself up."

I look down at my clothes, now soaking wet, and start laughing. The day's emotions have finally caught up to me and I feel myself crack. I laugh so hard until there is no noise coming from my mouth, only crying silent tears of pain. Shaun starts laughing with me, still with his hand over his eyes. "Why are you laughing so much?" he barely gets out.

"You threw my clean clothes, not a towel," I cry out. Shaun laughs harder, then slumps to the floor. As his butt lands on the floor, the towel that was hanging on the hook falls on top of his head.

"Found the towel, Fruit Loop." His voice is muffled by the towel.

I crawl forward and quickly pull it from his head, covering my body with it. His eyes are squeezed shut. "You can open your eyes now. I am covered up." I give him a lopsided smile which he returns.

"Not where I thought I would be twenty-four hours ago." I nod and then smile again, unable to stop myself.

"Yep," I say, popping the *p*. "If you'd have said *in twenty-four hours, you're gonna be sat in a dingy motel room with a complete stranger, only covered in a towel, with a sore hip,* I would have called the cops on you."

I go to stand up and Shaun's hands are already out to help me up. I hear him inhale and I look up at him.

"At least you smell good after all that." Then he winks at me, and butterflies erupt in my stomach.

Chapter 9 – Shaun.

Turning the shower off, I turn back to face her.

She's fucking beautiful.

It's the only thought going around in my head. She's standing in the shower, dripping wet, smelling like me, and it's driving my dick stir crazy.

Get it together, man.

"Shaun," she whispers.

"Yeah," I quietly mumble back, while staring into her eyes.

"Can you look at my hip, please?" Her cheeks are red, and she bites her lower lip.

Reaching up, I pull her lip away from her teeth with my thumb, sliding my hand across to cup her cheek. I feel my whole-body surge with the need to kiss her, to hold her. Staring at her lips, fixated on every little move she makes, I watch her tongue flick out to wet them. And my dick strains in my sweatpants as a result. Sliding my free hand down her back, I ask in a husky voice, "Which hip hurts?"

She gulps loudly, then reaches her arm around her to grab my hand, sliding it across her back and down to her hip without breaking eye contact with me. My dick painfully swells, and I'm sure if she dropped her head, she would see it. I wait, desperately hoping for her hand to move, to touch it.

"This one," she whispers again when my hand is in position on her hip.

I nod my head once and let go of her face, slowly crouching down until my knees hit the wet, tiled floor. I pull on her towel a little bit to the side to see her sore hip. The towel slips from her other side, revealing her gorgeously toned ass to me. My heart accelerates wildly, and I find myself starving for air. *For her.*

Slowly gliding my fingers across the already forming black bruise on her hip, I lean forward and drop a kiss on her skin. Gasping, she lets out a small moan. *Does she want this as much as me?*

I lean forward and kiss her hip again.

"*Shaun*," she moans out, her legs trembling in front of me with need. *She's like pure ecstasy.*

I feel my urge for her swell more and I ask her gravelly, "Tell me what you want, Brim."

"You," she begs as my hand gently pulls her towel down to the floor. Standing naked in front of me, my whole body grows feverish for her. I need to touch her, taste her, feel her tight pussy clench around me as I fuck her. Standing back up, she lets out a frustrated sigh and I smile. Scooping her up into my arms, I carry her bridal- style into the bedroom, before gently placing her down on the bed.

"Lights, madam?" I say and point to the once fully functioning fairy-lights on the Christmas tree in the corner.

"Please."

I turn and flick them on, and they gently twinkle multi colour sparkles around the room.

Pulling my shirt over my head, I spin round to face her. I wink at her reaction to my top half and stalk towards the foot of bed. "You're something else, you know that?" I tell her. She waves me off playfully. I stop, mesmerised for a moment, to watch her skin glittering in the glow of the lights twinkling behind me.

My eyes zone in on her full breasts as her breathing quickens, making them raise and fall rapidly. "How so?" she smirks.

"You're easily the most infuriating woman I've ever met." I pause to grab her ankles and gently spread her legs wide. "What a charmer," she mocks.

"But" I raise a brow at her, "you're easily the sexiest woman I've ever had in bed."

Sliding my hand up her leg, I kiss and lick my way from her ankles to her sensitive area as she moans and wriggles beneath my touch.

"Are you sure about this, Fruit Loop?" I quiz, wanting to make she really does want it.

"Yes, yes, please," she begs.

I slide my mouth across her pussy, groaning when her sweet honey juices land on my tongue. "Fuck, you taste good." Sliding my tongue up and down between the folds of her delicious cunt, she moans my name repeatedly as she chases down her climax. Hearing her calling out my name flicks a switch inside me, and I slowly run the palm of my hand over her stomach. I hold her firmly in place before attending to her pussy like it's my last meal, my grip on her growing more possessive and intense when she finally comes all over my tongue, over and over again.

Chapter 10 – Brim.

Fluttery sensations rush through my core—I've long forgotten the pain in my hip.

I scream out Shaun's name once more before he snaps and stands up, his hands fumbling at his waistband as he rips his grey sweatpants off. "Fuck, Brim, look what you're doing to me, doll."

I smile, still sated from the multiple orgasms he's given me. His cock springs free and I freeze, snapping out of my abyss.

"Shaun, that's..." I pause, flustered and shocked. "That's not–" I'm still unable to gather a coherent sentence.

He laughs while ripping the top of a condom wrapper with his teeth.

"Relax, Brim." He positions himself above me after rolling on the condom. "Trust me," he soothes.

He gently places a kiss on my shoulder before peppering me with them along my collarbone and up to my neck, moving to nibble at my ear lobe. Whispering between kisses along my jaw, "So beautiful."

I nuzzle my nose against the side of his head, wanting those lips on mine, and he smirks. "Be patient, Brimley." I huff at him, sliding my hands up and down his muscled arms, kissing him back on his neck. "Are you ready?" he asks. I feel his tip at my entrance, and I push my hips forward to let him know I am ready.

"Words, Brim." I snap my gaze up to him and nod once before telling him, "Yes, I'm ready."

His lips slam into mine, devouring my mouth like he is starving for me. Our teeth clash, and tongues dance as both of us explore one another. Feeling him slowly enter me and I dig my nails into his shoulders as the sting intensifies and tears prick my eyes. I've never been with anyone this big before. He takes it slowly, inching in little by little, before stopping to let me adjust to him. My painful moans turn into pleasurable ones and our bodies begin to move as one.

I moan loudly and he picks up the pace. My hand claws at his back as Shaun's groans become more frequent, and I feel the pull draw deep within my stomach. I am chasing my high.

"Let go, Brimley. Drench me. Drench my fucking cock." That was all I needed to tip me over the edge.

My whole body becomes weak, my legs opening wider as I wrap them around his waist. I scream his name into the night.

Chapter 11 – Shaun.

The morning light beams through the curtains in the motel room.

Yesterday, I didn't really notice how bad this place was. Stains cover the walls, the nets that hang in the window have rips in them, the wicker chair in the corner has seen better days.

A few days ago, I'd have been calling the motel inspector out to condemn the place. But right now, I don't give a fucking shit.

I cover Brim back up with the cover as she stirs beside me, her long brown hair spread out over the pillow as she snuggles herself further into my side. Gently moving a small strand of her hair, I push it behind her ear.

The effect she's had on me since she bumped into me at the airport in Paris... Well, let's say it's been a while since anyone has made me feel this way. I'm not the dating type. I don't do girlfriends, mainly because I'm a loner, but I enjoy that. I am content in my own space, in my own head. Truthfully, I enjoy my own company. I don't think I've ever dated any woman who has been okay with that in the past.

Last night though, damn, it's one I won't forget in a while. I really did mean it in a good way when I said she's something else. Brimley's a breath of fresh air; she's kind and caring. She could have flicked me off yesterday and told me to stick it where the sun doesn't shine, but she didn't. Fruit Loop doesn't judge.

What happens now? With us?

"I can hear the cogs turning in that head of yours, you know," her sleepy voice says. I smile down at her. "Sorry," I mutter.

"What are you thinking about?" she asks, while wrapping her arm around my waist and throwing her leg over mine. *You* is what I wanna say but stop myself.

"That train. I think I'm gonna head over to the motel reception and see if they have word yet. Try and grab some food for us while I'm at it."

She looks up at me with a frown on her face. "Oh, okay," she says, her tone sad.

"What's wrong, Brim?" I ask, while lifting my hand up to cup her cheek.

She stares into my eyes a little longer before

responding. "Happy Christmas Eve, Mr Grinch."

"You had to go there, didn't you?" I smirk before tickling her side.

Yelping out in pain, she jumps. "Ouch!" she cries out and I throw the covers back to look at her hip.

Shit, I'd forgotten about that. Fuck, what if I'd caused more damage last night? I should have taken her to the hospital, not fucked her.

"Shaun, it's okay. It's just a little sore, that's all. I'm okay," she tries to reassure me but I'm already looking over her skin. The bruise that was forming last night has now fully come out in a black and blue mark, covering her cream skin from the top of her leg up to her ribs on one side. I feel my heart racing. There's no way that's from her slipping in the shower... *I've definitely made it worse.*

"Shit, Brim, I'm sorry. Did I hurt you last night?" I say nervously.

Running her hand through her hair, she sighs heavily. "No, you buffoon, you did not. I would have told you, okay? I am fine, it's just the bruising, that's all. N ow, please come here and kiss me before you go and get me food." She winks with one eye and then the other. "Please? You owe me. Seeing as you kept stealing the covers all night. You know you're like fighting a bear to get them back, right?" she adds, then throws her arms out for me to embrace her.

I poke fun at her with a huge smile beaming on my face. "You fought with many bears?"

"That's really my job. I lied to you; I'm a professional bear fighter." She snickers, then holds her arms out wider and I lay down next to her snuggling my head into her neck. Using a free hand, I pull her leg over my body.

"As you wish. But I want you to know, I like being wrapped up like a burrito when I sleep, so, sue me." She giggles against my neck, and I drop a kiss on her cheek.

Her hand gently stokes through my mop of mousy blonde hair, and she gently whispers into my ear, "You mentioned food earlier."

My chuckle rumbles through my chest against her. "I meant me. I am food."

Chapter 12 – Brim.

It's surprising what sex can do for you. You know?

Yesterday my heart felt like it was desperate to get out of its cage from fear, but today it beats erratically for him. Every look he gives me, every soft touch of his hand, I feel my insides leap.

Still weird to think I've just met him, but at the same time, it's like we've known each other for years.

Maybe this was supposed to happen? This is how I'm meant to meet the one?

I stop moving towards the train to give myself a shake. I'm getting way, way ahead of myself here.

Making a mental note in my head I remind myself that.

1. I 've only known him a full forty-eight hours.
2. I don't know him, other than knowing he's a winemaker and owns a shop in

Manhattan, and that he has a younger brother called Jack.

3. He hogs the covers in bed.
4. He is hard to gauge and loses patience quickly.
5. He hates Christmas.
6. Yes, he may be a God in the sheets, but he could still be a freak out of them.
7. He loves his own space. Once the initial attraction has worn off, I'll turn into a lonely old spinster lady who only sees her man at mealtimes, if that.
8. I'm just a normal girl who had a one-night stand. Nothing more can come of it. Once we arrive in New York, he will go his own way and I will go mine. No inevitable heart aches. *Simple.*
9. What happened in the motel room, can stay in the motel room.

Once I have wild emotions in check, I continue my walk to the train. The tracks are now clear and, touch wood, we should be okay for a smooth rest of the journey home. I catch up to Shaun, but when he goes to reach for my hand, I rush to put it in my pocket.

What happened in the motel room, stays in the motel room.

His eyes flash with hurt and his brows furrow down. Shuffling his steps, he lets out an audible sigh. "You, okay?" he asks.

Pinching my lips together, I look up at him and nod, before looking ahead again since unsure what else to say. Walking the rest of the route in silence, I zone in on my footing as the snow crunches beneath my feet.

Helping me to my seat, he points toward the toilets in the carriage and doesn't return to me for the rest of the journey.

Chapter 13 – Shaun.

J ust like that, she shook me off. After getting what she wanted, a place to stay for the night and a good fuck, she turns away from me.

I am tired of asking her if she's okay. I seem to do it a lot. After watching her dart her hand into her pocket when I went to help her through the snow, I quickly put it all together in my head. *She doesn't want to know me.*

So, butthurt, I nodded towards the toilet s and decided at that moment to sit somewhere else.

Flicking through my phone I check in on some supplier s' emails, replying to them to inform them I will be returning to work the day after tomorrow, and anything else can wait until then. I try to think of anything on the way back to New York to distract myself from facing my father later tonight and Brim being a carriage away from me now, but nothing works, so I close my eyes and let sleep take over.

∞∞∞

I wake to Brim sitting next to me on the train reading a book. It takes me a moment to realise she's wearing nothing but panties and a bra with a Santa's hat on her head.

"Brim, what are you doing?" I groggily ask, gesturing to her outfit of choice. Granted, it's way better than the light up *I heart Xmas* sweater and bright green leggings, but the protective, jealous side of me takes over and I don't like the other passengers looking at her, mainly the men, the way they are right now.

"What do you mean?" she grins.

I huff out my annoyance, wondering if she hit her head when she fell in the shower last night, and pull my puffer jacket off to dress her in. "You're practically naked on a train full of passengers, Brimley!" I seethe through gritted teeth.

"Oh, this?" she waves her hands up and down her body, placing her book back in her bag. "Well, I figured I owed you an apology for earlier and thought you prefer me like this." She pauses to push her glasses up the bridge of her nose. "I was going to dress up like a present so you could unwrap me, but that seemed like too much effort and he–" She stops to point at my dick straining in my pants, begging to be set free. "Looks like he'd have agreed with me." She smirks then rises to her feet, placing her hands on my shoulders as she pushes me back down until my ass lands on the chair. She starts to undo my belt buckle and looks up at me through her lashes. Biting her lower lip, she asks, "Are you ready for your present now, Santa?"

I nod slowly. "Abso-fucking-lutley, Brim. Santa's ready." Lifting my hips for brim to pull my pants down, not giving a single fuck that the whole train can see my dick springing free, Brim licks the tip to the bottom. She hums in response to my precum taste on her tongue and I let out a loud groan with her name trembling off my lips.

"SHAUN! SHAUN!" I'm being shaken awake by my shoulders, and I mumble out Brim's name.

"Shaun, wake the fuck up!" I hear Brim's voice cry out as I'm slapped across the face.

"What?" I say, then it hits me. *Fuck, I was dreaming. That seemed so fucking real.* My heart leaps from my chest and my eyes fly open. Brim's looking down at me, her face flushed and concerned.

"Shit." I curse a few more times, clutching my chest as Brim controls her breathing beside me. I can't look at her or anywhere else on the train, so I look outside the window, seeing New York's famous skyscrapers not too far into the distance. *Fuck, does she suspect I was having the filthiest dream about her giving me head right here in the spot?* I look down between my legs to see my dick rock hard underneath my pants. Grabbing my jumper from my bag, I put it over my trousers. *Think of something quick, you twit. Go floppy now.* I need a cold shower pronto.

"Okay." I hear Brim sigh beside me. I glance over and see her hands as she drums her fingers on her legs, before rubbing them up and down her jeans.

"So, you good, yeah?" she asks, not looking at me, her eyes focused on the seat in front of her.

I clear my throat and shake my head, grimacing embarrassedly that she knows I was having a dirty dream about her. *Deny, deny, deny, if she ever asks.*

"Yep"

Brim takes a sharp inhale of air into her nose and stands up. "Good, as long as you're not hurt, Santa," she says and then quickly walks off. I slide further down into my seat and wipe the sweat dripping from down my forehead away with my jacket that was covering my hard- on. She *100% knows.*

Chapter 14 – Brim.

The train finally comes to a halt at Central Station.

I practically sprint off the train as quickly as I can. *I'M HOME!* is what I want to scream at the top of my lungs as I run through the station towards the exit. *I finally made it back.* Weaving in and around crowds of people on my way to get outside, the cool breeze hit s my face first as I get closer to the main entrance, before the typical smell of smoke, weed and pollution fully invade my nostrils. I smile widely.

Thankfully, the painkillers I took thirty minutes ago have kicked in, and now the pain in my hip feels okay; it will be enough to keep me going until Mom can take a look at it.

In forty minutes, I'll be hugging my mom and dad—tears well in my eyes at the thought of seeing them all again. I wrap my jacket around me tighter as I stand to hail a cab down. *Christmas can really begin now.*

I stand waiting with my hand in the air as whistles and car horns can be heard around me. Dropping my hand momentarily to text Franny to let everyone know I'll be home in the next hour, and of course demanding she get the largest bottle of wine open for me, I put my phone away in the back of my jeans pocket, waving desperately at a few taxi drivers, hoping one will stop for me.

That's the problem with New Yorkers: if you're a cab driver, you've been around the block enough times to know who the tourists are, and if they are despicable enough, they will stop by for them. These poor people don't know they are about to be scammed out of more dollars than they're supposed to pay.

Thankfully though, a driver stops in front of me, leaning his head down to look at me through his open window. "You getting in, lady?" His broad accent fills my ears and I jump up, shouting yes excitedly.

As I pull my suitcase behind me, and the cab driver gets out to assist me putting it in the trunk and I hear my cab door shut.

My anger rises to boiling point, and I pull open the door, trying not to wince too much at the pain in my side. "Who do you think you are, huh?" I shout, peering into the cab. M y eyes widen when I see who it is, and I point my finger right in his stupid face. "You son of a bitch!" I slam the door shut, and stamp my foot into the ground, clenching my fists either side of me.

The cab driver stands next to me, asking if I'm okay. "Yes, I'm fine. Can you please just take me to Garden Place, Brooklyn?" Yanking back on the door, I rip it open, jumping into my seat. I fix Shaun with a cold glare. He smiles crookedly at me and my lips curl. "You," I shout, then point in his face again. "You need to tell him where you're going now!" He jumps at my tone and looks down at his hands in his lap.

I'm acting hysterically, I know, but I'm so goddamn angry. Not only does he sit away on the train after we slept together and spent the night with each other, but he also shouts my name sexily in his sleep, making everyone laugh at him on the train. A nd now the asshole is trying to steal my fucking taxi! *Deep breaths, Brim. Deep, calm breaths.* "I'm going to Brooklyn too," he says quietly as his ears turn red and he begins to fiddle with his watch on his wrist.

Looking up at the taxi driver who's grinning up at us in the rear-view mirror, I narrow my eyes. "You heard him; we are both going to Brooklyn," I snap.

Chuckling to himself, he tips his peaked hat. "Yes, m a'am," he says to me, then puts the cab into drive and we pull off into the traffic ahead.

"You're mad at me?" Shaun asks.

"Yes, you're a big fucking jerk face!" I angrily shout, instant regret panging in my chest as I glance up at him. He's still looking down at his watch, just nodding his head. He looks defeated. I want to comfort him, but I stop myself. My hands shake and I clamp my jaw shut. It's for the best, I tell myself.

He likes the quiet life that only involves him, and I like the big and loud, crazy, in your face, kind of life. We are completely opposite. *I think?*

We sit in awkward silence for a few minutes. I look out the window, watching as we pass the brightly lit streets of the city. Every shop window is covered with Christmas decorations. Carollers stand on the sidewalks singing Christmas songs, last minute shoppers pile out of stores with bags loaded up. It really is an amazing time of the year. That is, taking away a redirected flight, a broken-down train, no motel rooms, a one-night stand, and then an uncomfortable cab ride all with the same guy you cannot seem to shake away in person and in mind.

"I'm sorry," I say, turning my body towards him. He flexes his jaw and rubs the back of his neck, still not wanting to make eye contact with me. "I really am, Shaun. I guess I am just so overwhelmed and emotional from the last few days. It's all getting to me the closer I am to home; it has been a lot for us both, hasn't it?" I say quietly, hoping he will look at me.

Turning his head towards the window, I hear him whisper, "*Home,*" then nothing more. Tears start to fill my eyes again and my vision blurs. I turn my head the other way to look out the window and cover my mouth with my sleeve, closing my eyes so he can't see or hear me cry silently beside him.

Chapter 15 – Shaun.

She's right to be mad at me, I guess, but I have every right to be mad at her too. Well, right now, I'm not angry. I'm lost for words, trying to get my head around why this hurts.

Let's just say, I'm not ready to say goodbye.

I know I'm arduous work to be around. I know I fly off the handle. I'm not perfect in any way. I want to tell her this, but not when she's angry with me.

Opening my bag in between my legs in the footwell of the cab, I find my wallet, pulling it out from the bag. Flicking through my cards, I find what I'm searching for.

I grab my business card, thankful I always have one to hand, and look over at her. She's turned away from me, looking out the window beside her. Spotting her bag separating us in the middle seat, I notice it's open. Moving slowly to not alert her, I drop my card into it.

Maybe later, she will find it, and when she's ready, we can talk.

At this moment, today of all days, I need to stay focused on putting a brave, confident face on, to walk into my parent's home.

Part of me longs to ask Brim to come with me; not to use as a shield against my dad, but more of a calming tool for me. Having her beside me would give me something, *someone*, else to focus on, but for two reasons I can't bring myself to do it— one, she's not talking to me, and two, I'd be too scared of my dad turning on her.

The fact we barely know each other doesn't scare me. Every couple in every relationship all over the world was at this point. *It's just the case of seeing if she's ready for that.*

We cross over Dumbo bridge and my heart picks up pace. The cab's going to stop soon for her, and I don't know if I will ever see her again. In my peripheral vision, I see her fidgeting with her sweater sleeve. I pinch my lips together to stop myself from smiling — at least it's not a light up one.

This one's bright red, covered in reindeers. Memories of last night in the motel room spring to mind; me sitting on the bed as she giggled at my impression of the crazy lady on the plane. I called her a deer trapped in the headlights. I waited for her to make her move. At the time, it never crossed my mind that I was going to end up fucking her.

I thought I had my lust under control. But really, thinking about it, I wouldn't change last night or this horrible journey back here for a thing.

The cab comes to a stop after Brim asks him to pull over on the side of Garden Place Road. Shuffling around in her seat, she grabs her phone from her back pocket and, leaning forward to tap the contactless pay screen before I can stop her, pays the fare.

"I'd have paid, Brim," I say, grabbing her arm gently.

She turns slowly to look down at my hand on her arm and I use my free hand to place my pointer finger under her chin, pulling her head up to look at her.

Her face is damp from shed tears, and her beautiful brown eyes are now red from crying. I want to kiss her so badly, but I can't. One day she will find my card. I just hope when the time comes, she will call.

I stare into her eyes, pleading with her in my mind to stay. *Don't leave me just yet or ask me to come with you.*

She reaches up her hand to brush along my jaw with her fingers. T ears drop onto her cheeks, and she bites her wobbling bottom lip. I kiss her forehead. "Brim." My voice is a new sound to me, cracked and quiet. She leans forward and drops a gentle, almost feather like kiss on my lips and whispers her

71

goodbye.

Fuck not kissing her. I lean forward and slam my mouth on her lips, her salty tears seeping between our locked mouths. For what feels like the tenth time during this trip, I pray to God in my head.

'This time I mean it. I know I'm not a religious man, but fuck, if you need me to go to church, I will. Just please let me keep her.'

Breaking our kiss, she pulls back, her voice breaking as she mutters, "Bye, Grinchy" and attempts to give me her best fake smile. She fails as more tears fall, but she collects her bag and closes the door.

The taxi driver had already gotten out of the cab before we kissed and went to the trunk to get her suitcase. He hands it to her, and she thanks him before spinning on her feet and walking down the street. She doesn't look back once.

The driver's door closes, and I'm forced to look towards him. He tugs at the collar on his shirt and weakly smiles, saying, "That was intense. Where to man?"

Staring him down, I tell him, "The Merlot Man, please."

I need some peace and time to myself. One thing I can't face now is walking through the doors of my childhood home. The party doesn't start until seven. By the time I get to my wine store, I'll have two hours to kill before I need to head over there.

"Thank you. Keep the change." I wave off the cab driver and throw one strap of my rucksack over my shoulder and pick up my holdall from the floor. My store has always been my comfort zone; I come here to chill.

Flipping the keys around to find the one that opens the side door rather than the main one, I flick the lock and open it up, dropping my bags as the sudden strong wine scents from all over the store hit me. I take one deep, long breath in.

Grabbing a bottle of my best and most popular choice wine from the shelf, twisting the cap off and downing a mouth full of it. The rich and strong fruity taste of berries hits the back of my throat, and my body relaxes. *This* is my home.

Stumbling out of the cab at my parent 's house on the night of my younger brother's engagement party wasn't my greatest idea. But we move forward.

Welcome to hell. How does it finally feel to be back?

I trip up the stairs, stopping at the top step to regain my posture, not that it really works. I sway back and forth on my legs, feeling the sickly taste of bile rise in my throat. *Fuck, I'm gonna throw up.*

I lean up against the stone wall near the front door as my vision dances bright circles in front of me. My temperature rises and I rip my suit jacket off. Wrapping my arms around my stomach as I bend down, throwing up all over the Merry Christmas door mat my mother had put out. *SHIT.*

My dad chooses that exact moment to open the front door. I look up at him and smile my sickly smile at him, and he covers his mouth and nose with his sleeve. "For fuck's sake, Shaun! What is wrong with you?" I hiccup in his face, and he stumbles back. I let out a hearty laugh and wobble towards the door, stepping in my own vomit then tracking it all through the hallway, as guests gasp in horror. *Whoops.*

I hear my dad shouting at me again, but I keep walking, flicking him the middle finger over my shoulder. My mom tuts and pulls me into the kitchen.

"Jesus, Shaun, what have you gone and done with yourself now?" She soothes me, rubbing my back and guiding me to the kitchen table.

"Heeeee don't deserve you, Mom," I slur out to her.

"Shhh now, let's get you some water and into bed."
I feel her undoing the laces on my shoes and taking them off.

Jack's blurry face comes into view. He's grinning.
"Hey there, big bro. What an entrance." He chuckles and I smile at him. "Your breath fucking stinks though. You finally raided your own cellar, I see." He picks up one of my arms and hauls me up onto my feet, wrapping my arm around his shoulders and his arm around my back. "Take him to bed, Jack. I'll go deal with your father," Mom says before kissing us both on the cheek.

"He's an asshole," I tell Jack.

"Yeah, well, now you know where you get it from," Jack mumbles back as he drags my body up the stairwell. I force him to stop at the top of the stairs. I look him the best I can in the eye. "I'm sorry if I ruined yours and Kimmy's night."

He smiles up at me "Don't sweat it. It was kind of boring speaking to all of Dad's friends anyway." Adding a wink. "I get why you're like this tonight though. Now don't get all sappy on me. Come on, let's get you to bed."

"Goooood morning! You know you're getting coal

in your sack, right?" Jack shouts, making my head pound in pain.

I squint my eyes as he flings open my bedroom curtains. "Please, Jack," I plead. "Just one more minute." My throat burns with acid, and I sit up too quickly to grab the glass of water by my bed. Thankfully, Jack's there to grab the glass before it slips, and I flop back down. "Urrghh," I groan.

"You'd rather me be waking you up, trust me," he says in a low, warning tone.

"I'm sure I would. Since when did you take on the big bro role, though?" I grin at him as he passes me the glass of water. Suddenly I feel like I'm dying of thirst and drain the cold glass contents down in one gulp.

"Since you barely come home or over to my place anymore. I don't see you or hear from you. I know whatever happens when you walk down those stairs today will most likely end in you walking right out the front door. I guess if looking after your hungover ass is what I got to do to spend some time with you before all that happens, then yeah, it looks like now I'm taking on the role." He looks over at me sadly and guilt pangs in my chest.

We used to be so close; he was, and easily still is, my best friend. My favourite days as a kid were when we would go cycling around Brooklyn, just the two of us. My best memory was one hot summer's day in Prospect Park; we were down near the pond, and

Jack was demanding I lay down on this floating plank, as he called it— it was a large chunk of wood. I did as he asked after much deliberation, getting in the water, and laying down on the plank, then watching him as he dived into the water.

He came up to the side of my plank and pointed at it. "This is a door, okay?" I grinned. "Oookay," I said, waiting for him to explain the aim of the game to me.

"I'm Jack, and you're Rose. I need you to shake my arm and tell me there's a boat, Jack, there's a boat. Okay?" He grinned up at me as excitement sparked in his eyes.

"Well, why can't I be in the water, and you shake my arm?" I quizzed.

He rolled his eyes. "Because in the film *Titanic,* does it speak of the man being Shaun Dawson? Rose doesn't lay there saying, *Shaun, there's a boat! There's a boat, Shaun!* Does she? Huh, no, she does not. And it was Jack Dawson that she called to. Lucky for me, I was born Jack Dawson too, so you lose. Now shake my arm and cry!"

We laughed for hours, jumping in and out of the water that day. We grew tired after a while and decided to get out and go fetch ice cream.

As I laid on the plank, Jack, the little shit, flipped the piece of wood from under neath and I fell in the water, coughing and sputtering as I gulped down a mouth full of it. He, of course, thought this was hilarious; I glared at him. He dipped his head into the pond, taking a mouthful of water and swallowing it down. "See, stop being a baby!" he said while pointing at me.

"Fish poop in that all day, you know," I told him, smiling wickedly, knowing the idea of fish poo swimming around in his stomach would give me the last laugh. He gagged dramatically. "You're just jealous they named the main character after me," Jack snapped as he stuck out his tongue, rubbing his shirt over the top to get the water out of his mouth.

"No, they did not. You were named after that character. That film's hundreds of years old, its Momma's favourite film, dummy," I told him, wrapping my arms around him before knuckle rubbing the top of his head, then running off to get my bike.

I snap out my memories when he lays next to me on the bed. "You know I'm sorry, right?" I say, tapping him on his chest with the back of my hand.

He laughs out loud, "Yeah, I know, but–" he pauses to roll on to his side to face me. "If you pull a stunt like last night at my wedding, I'll kick your fucking ass, got it?" I quietly huff a laugh and nod my head. "You have my word. I will behave."

He smiles at me. "Good, because you're the best man. You can bring Brimley as your plus one, you know," he announces as he rolls back over on to his back and stares up at the ceiling with a huge grin on his face. It takes a second for me to click on to what he just said.

"Wait, what? You want me to be your best man? What about Jasper? And how'd you know about Brim?" I practically shout, wide eyed, at him. I'm filled with joy that he wants me to be his best man over the guy he's best friends with his whole life, but also shocked he wants me to be. I've been a shit brother to him over the last few years. Not in a mean way, I just closed him out. It was easier that way.

"Yeah, I want you to be my best man. You're my brother, and everyone knows— *apart from you clearly*— that brother code stands higher than the bestie code. Trust me on this." He turns his head to look at me. "Now, you gonna tell me about Santa's little helper you kept banging on about in bed last night, or not?" I cannot help but smile widely at him calling Brim *Santa's little helper*. So, I tell him about the last few days, every detail, in the best *PG* rated way I can. He listens intently, stopping me occasionally to bark out laughing.

...

"So, what happened yesterday after she got out the cab? She must have seen the card in her bag by now. How big was her bag?" His brows furrow, and he waves his hands around as gets up from the bed pacing. He mutters to himself a plan to knock on every door on the street the cab driver dropped her off at until we find her. "I'll let fate decide if I hear or see her again," I tell him calmly.

"What?" he shouts, stopping to face me with his hands in his hair. "Noooo, you have to find her; she's the one for you, don't you see it?" I laugh, not because his wild and crazed look is funny— well, it is — but because I know he is right. The fact that he is not telling me to run for the hills, screaming at me she's a raving nutjob speaks volumes. "Yeah, I see it, pal. You will be the first to know if it happens."

A knock comes from the other side of my bedroom door, and the calmness I felt the last hour with Jack depletes. I know who's on the other side and this time, I'm ready to give him a piece of my mind. It's time he knows exactly how I feel.

Chapter 16 – Brim.

Tears keep pouring down my face as I retell the story of my journey from Paris to home. My dad and mom sit either side of me on the couch, while my five sisters sit on the floor in front of me; they all wear the same sad expression on their faces. "So, after I got out the cab, I walked away," I sob. "Why does it hurt so much? I don't get it; I don't even know him! This is a crazy way to act."

Nobody says a word for a while; they all just take it in turns to switch places rubbing my back and kissing my head.

"You still have a shovel, right, Dad?" Rory, one of my five sisters, asks.

"How about some cable ties, Dad?" Lottie is the next one to ask him.

Abbey looks at Rory and Lottie with a grin before adding, "And duct tape, D ad. You must have some of that!"

"Oooh, D ad, I know we will need some bleach!" Franny shouts.

"The hacksaw, Father" Annie laughs out.

"I have all those things." My dad turns to me. "We got an address for this guy? Your sisters and I are ready to rock and roll."

"Please don't forget alibis— you all were here, okay? All night, watching that *Die Hard* movie," Mom softly adds, then winks at me, and I start to laugh at my beautifully weird family. It is so good to be back with them.

∞∞∞

"Hey, you, okay?" Franny asks as her head pops around my bedroom door, holding two bottles of Dad's beer in her hand. Out of my five sisters, Francesca is the one I'm closest to.

Franny is the oldest by one year. She is the bad ass one of the family, drives the motorbike, has tattoos all over her body.

Then, it is me: the apparent lovesick, eccentric one.

The twins, Abbey, and Annie are next, both two years younger than me and they couldn't be more different. It is crazy to think they are twins; if you ever saw them standing next to one another, you wouldn't believe it.

Abbey's the sporty one: she loves running, hockey, football. Annie is the emo one of the group; black feeds her soul, at least that is what she likes to inform us of occasionally.

Lottie is up next. She's a year younger than the twins. She's the fashionable diva and hates with a passion when Annie and I are in the same room—my bright clothes and the contrast of Annie's dark ones, give her a migraine.

And last but not least, the baby of the family, a.k.a the mistake, Rory— she's the prankster of the house.

They are the biggest bunch of pains in the asses, but I love them all deeply.

I smile at Franny. "Yeah, all good in the hood."

Franny raises a brow and steps inside my room, closing the door behind her. "You know, I don't think anyone says that anymore." She sits down on the bed next to me and hands me a bottle. "You wanna tattoo? I have gotten good at doing them now, see," she pulls up the sleeve of her top to reveal a small stack of books on her left wrist.

"That's so cute, I love that! Maybe one day I'll let you, just not yet" I say biting my lip.

Nodding her head, she takes a swig of her beer. "This is the needle thing again, right?" she asks, cocking her head to one side to gauge my answer.

My cheeks burn up and my heart races at the idea of needles being jabbed into my body. I really don't understand her enjoyment of it. "Maybe," I grumble, pushing at her shoulder.

"So, I've been looking online, and I accidently *on-purpose* stumbled on a website I think you should take a look at," she tells me while bending over the side of my bed to look under it.

Pulling out my laptop, she sits up straight in my bed, typing away. She pulls up the page, turning the screen away at the last second so I can't see it. "Don't freak the fuck out on me but hear me out for a second." She grabs one of my hands in hers.

"I met a guy at my motorcycle club. His name is Heath. He was smart, caring, dirty," she winks, and I smile at her. "So, *so* handsome. I spent the entire summer with him one year. We rode down to Florida, spent days on the beach and nights in cocktail bars, dancing like no one else was there, just him and me. We would kiss passionately, and we loved each other hard. He was everything to me." Tears well in her eyes, leaving me speechless again for the second time in the space of a few days. "I miss him, Brim."

Shuffling my butt across the bed closer to her, I wrap my arm around her back and hook my hand onto her shoulder, pulling her into my side. "What happened?" I whisper.

"He left that summer once it had ended. He wanted to travel the world and I wasn't ready for it. We said our goodbyes at the airport, and I promised him I'd wait for him to return." She looks up at me, her eyes puffy, her chin trembling. "That was four years ago. I know in my gut he's not coming back." She fans her face while sitting up straight, pulling the laptop onto her lap. "Like I said, don't freak out, but I don't want you to suffer the pain like I did. Sometimes I still do." she turns the screen and I close it slightly before seeing what's on it.

Taking her hand back in mine, I tip my chin to her. "Only if you promise me right now, swear on the baby Jesus, that you will talk to me if you're ever in pain, okay?" She nods, looping her baby finger in mine. "I pinkie promise." Getting up from the bed, she grabs her bottle of beer.

As she reaches my bedroom door, she says, "Call him Brim. don't let him get away if he's really the one."

Chapter 17 – Shaun.

"**S**it," he orders, pointing to the chair sat opposite his desk.

I slump down into it, adjusting my posture to sit with my forearms laid along my legs and my hands clasped together at the knees.

"Talk," he demands, before picking up a stack of papers on his desk and flicking through them.

He hasn't even got the decency to talk to me face to face.

"What do you want to know?" I bite out, my blood quickly boiling up.

"Explain last night for me." He looks up from the paper in his hand at me, completely blank of emotion.

"I got fucking drunk. I needed a pick- me- up. Not only did my plane back from Paris get rerouted, but my train broke down, the motel room looked like a crack house, the taxi ride home fucking sucked." My anger is rising by the second. I stand and stroll over to his desk. "You wanna know why I got so fucking wasted last night, Dad, really?" He doesn't say a word, just looks through me like he's allowing me to get this out before he sends me on my way. "You," I point at him. "I can handle all that shit happening but what I can't take another day in my life is dealing with you!" I slam my fist into his desk "You have pushed me aside since I was a kid, treated me like I am not your own. All the times I had to pretend I wasn't in the room. But Jack?" I laugh. "The golden boy— he got everything. Fishing trips, holidays, everything he got was new and upgraded. I longed for you to treat me that way, but you did not."

"You taught him how to ride his bike, you remember that? You never made that time for me. Jack, my younger brother, had to teach me, *his older brother*, how to ride a goddamn bike because you would not do it." I take a moment to compose myself, keeping my eyes lasered in on a tea stain he has on his desk. "You weren't there for me. Even when I left this place, I should call home and started my own business, building it up from scratch, you never once told me you were proud of me or said congratulations. I worked my ass off, not only to get out of here and away from you, but a tiny part of me wanted to do it all *for* you. All, so you would tell me you knew I could do it, you're proud of me, or even acknowledge what you've done and apologise when you see how well I, not you, but *I* shaped my life."

His head is down, looking at his suit when I finish. I

stay quiet to see if he has anything at all to say, but not surprisingly, he doesn't.

I hear his office door open. Mom and Jack both stand on the other side, Mom with a look of fear on her face and Jack's solemn. I turn back to my father who hasn't even looked up to acknowledge their presence in the room. I tap the table and turn on my heel, walking out the room with my head high, before turning back at the door frame.

"The sad part about this, you had thirty years to see it, to spot it, and you didn't. You just kept putting me down, even when I had blatantly been crying, you didn't give a fuck. I went through hell to get here for this *magical* time of year, but I met the most amazing girl along the way, and I let her go. The woman who knew *instantly* how to make me feel complete, I watched walk away and I don't know if I'll ever find Brimley again. I did not come here for you if you're wondering; I did it for Jack and Mom."

"You don't need to worry about me, not anymore. I am not your problem, your fucking headache, any longer." My voice is hoarse. "I can stand on my own two feet just fine; I don't need a dad."

I trek upstairs to my room, grabbing boxes from mom's office along the way that I could use to fill my stuff up in, not that I want to take a lot of things from this room, but the memories I do have of Jack, mom, and me, I'll take. I hadn't quite expected to go off like that at him, least of all closing the door completely.

I don't feel empty though, or broken over it, just numb.

Merry Christmas to me.

I pack for a few hours, while Mom pesters me to stop and talk to her or eat. She handed me a box of unopened presents; I told her I would open them later when I felt more up to it, then she asked me about Brim, which I was more than happy to talk about.

Sitting on my bed, putting my feet up after loading the last bits of my things into Jack's car, I realize it's late afternoon. I wasn't going to load all my things up today but after catching Dad sitting at the top of the stairs, listening to my conversation with mom and Jack about Brim, I changed my mind.

I flick through emails when one catches my eye, subject lined: **You're Fired.** I frown, *what the fuck? Me? Fired from my own business?* By who?

Opening it up quickly, I read through it all.

Dear Mr Grinchy,

You mentioned you owned and worked at The Merlot Man in Manhattan; it didn't take me long to find your email address online.

*Sorry about the **you're fired** part above, I just wasn't sure if you'd read my email, so I had* *to make sure I had your attention.*

After you so kindly sleighed my bells Christmas Eve's Eve and then let me stay the night, I feel I owe you an explanation / apology for my sudden change of tune towards you.

I don't usually do that kind of thing if you get my ~~'snow'~~ drift. (wink face emoji)

I' m not the one-night stand kind of girl; I like to get to at least three dates before I carefully consider the idea of banging someone.

I have no idea where you live, nor do I have your number. I don't know if you like olives or what your favourite colour is. I don't know your birthday. How old are you? Do you like to watch movies or are you the party going person? (I don't think you are but then again, you might be). Do you usually have sexual dreams about women you've not long met on public transport, like is that a regular occurrence for you?

I have so many questions, I want to ask you...

The truth of the matter is, I don't know you. But I want to. There is so much I wished I had said to you in the taxi. I get you might be slightly freaked out after reading this and I completely get it if I don't hear from you.

But if you do and if you are ever free, would you like to go on a date sometime?

My number is (212) 658 9565.

*I hope you are having wine-derful
Christmas, Fruit Loop. Xoxo*

I smile from ear to ear, re-reading the email repeatedly; she wants a date. *Maybe God finally heard my prayers.* I huff out a laugh; she sent me this last night. Quickly saving her name and number in my phone, I can't wait any longer to text her.

Me – To answer some of your questions:

1. I am 30, born right here in NYC, March 22nd, putting me on the cusp of both Aries and Pisces.
2. Live in Manhattan above my wine store.
3. I hate olives.
4. My favourite colour is a deep red.
5. Stay indoors and watch movies, man, every time.
6. No, I have not ever, until the other morning on the train, had a sexual dream about any woman on public transport. So, no, it is not a regular thing for me.
7. I absolutely want to go on a date with you. How about tonight?
8. And now you have my number. Although you have had it for 24 hours— I slipped my business card into your bag, go take a look. (wink face emoji) xx

Her reply is instant.

Fruit Loop - Looking....xxx

Fruit Loop - When did you put that in my bag? xxx

Me - In the cab, yesterday, before you left me. XX

Fruit Loop is calling...

My heart races frantically in my chest, butterflies take flight in my stomach as her name dances across my screen. Hitting the green answer button as quickly as I can, I smile into the phone.

"Hey," I say, my voice cheery and light.

"Hey, Grinchy, I didn't think you'd ever reply to me." She sounds hurt and upset, so I quickly get my reply in.

"Yeah, well, I was beginning to believe you'd never find my card," I say, wishing I could reach into the phone to touch her.

"I can't believe you put your card in my bag; I emptied the thing out last night as well. It was stuck in the bottom of my bag, covered in a sticky candy cane wrapper." She giggles out the candy cane part.

"*Candy cane*...Why am I not surprised by that, Fruit Loop?" I pause as she laughs some more "Can I please come see you?" I ask, trying not to sound like the weak, desperate man I am for her.

"Sure. I live at forty-five garden place. Bring your wine," she softly tells me.

"Eureka, doll," I laugh aloud in pure bliss. "I will see you soon," I tell her, and she tells me goodbye before hanging up. I quickly fight my clothes off and jump into the shower, not wanting to waste another moment here.

Charging down the stairs, I take them two at a time, passing my dad in the hallway.

"Shaun?" The way he says my name makes me stop, although not enough to face him.

"You're leaving already?" he asks, his tone loss of all its aggression.

I grit my teeth, swiping my tongue along the top set. "Yeah, I have someone who actually does want to see me and spend time with me." I make my voice clear and sharp.

"Brimley."

"Keep her name out your mouth," I warn him, my whole body violently shaking.

"Shaun, it is not that I don't want to spend time with you, nothing like that. In fact, the complete opposite." I spin round, ready to give him round two, clenching my fists into balls at my side. *How dare he make out he wants me around!*

He holds his hand up, signalling me to wait for him to finish. His eyes are glossy as if he's been crying. I scrunch my nose up at him, nodding for him to go on.

"My dad, your grandfather, treated me like a prince. I had everything I ever needed, wanted." He clears his throat. "I was spoiled rotten. And I got away with absolutely everything, **every time**. If I messed up, he brushed it right under the carpet. Ignoring the way, I was. I knew I could do whatever I pleased. I got into trouble numerous times. Each time, he would bail me out of jail, and never once did I thank him." Tears begin to stream down his face. He snuffles and a small part that I kept hidden in a dark corner of my heart for him breaks.

"On his death bed, he told me he disliked me, the man I'd become, wished he was harder, wished he'd worked less to help my mother out with me." He sobs into his hands, and my mom comes out from the kitchen to soothe him, nodding for him to continue. I stand in front of him, rooted to the spot wanting to tell him not to continue if it hurts him this much, but on the other hand, I don't understand the way he's ever treated me.

He regains himself and looks me dead in the eye. "I made a vow that night to never treat you the way he treated me growing up. I wanted you to work for everything, I wanted you to become a man I wasn't. I figured if I was harder on you, then you would have more respect for family, friends, and school." He pauses, "And me. I hoped by doing that, you'd never turn out to be a spoilt, selfish brat like I was. But as always, I got it wrong. I agree with everything you said: I was much more lenient on Jack. I see the man you are, hardworking, kind, loyal to all around you and me."

He steps forward. "The day you went international with your winery was the proudest day of my life. I remember thinking, my boy's an adult, he doesn't need me to guide him any more I wish I could turn back the clock. I'd spend more time with you like a father and son should. With Jack, I wanted to enjoy it. You know, before he goes off into the world too, like you did." he gulps loudly. "I'm sorry, Shaun. Truly, I am."

My vision blurs from his admissions and I take a step back, angrily wiping the tears away from my face. I feel his arms wrap around my back and for the first time in years, I cry into his shoulder. "I'm so sorry, son."

Chapter 18 - Brim.

"So, when's the hunk of junk arriving" Lottie asks.

"I don't know. Hey, you think I look, okay?" I ask, not looking at her. Spinning from side to side in the dress she brought me for Christmas, it swishes around my knees.

"Yeaaaaah, you look cute!" she tells me, her tone sounding bored as she continues to stare down at her phone screen. I roll my eyes and turn back to the mirror. "Maybe it's too much."

Franny comes flying around Lottie's door frame. "H e's here, bitch! Get downstairs now before Dad answers the door." Panic sets inside me and I sprint towards the front door.

"Tell me you hid Dad's gun, right?" I call back to Franny who is hot on my tail.

"Wait, Dad has a gun? *Coooool*!" I hear Rory shout from behind me.

"*That's a negative*! I saw Dad load it up after you told him you had that male friend, who you were crying over when you arrived, coming round tonight," Annie sing songs up the stairs as we rush towards her. I halt in front of her, grabbing the sides Annie's face with my hands, squishing her lips together with my thumbs. "He did what now?"

Abbey bursts into laughter next to Annie and they bump fists. "We are totes joking with you!" Abbey says.

"Dads at the door, I repeat, Dad is at the door!" Rory shouts through a microphone behind us in the hallway. We all drop our heads, cursing how loud it is, making us cover our ears. *Where the fuck did, she get that from?*

"For God's sake, Rory, turn the volume down," Mom says as she snatches it out her hand to inspect the thing. I watch her for a second when her mouth turns slack, and she stares up at me.

"What?" I ask her. She drops the microphone on the floor and my sisters around me giggle.

"Mom, what is wrong? Is it my dress? It's too much isn't it" I say, looking down at it, contemplating if I have time to change.

I hear his voice before I see him, and everything clicks into place. My mom smiles widely at me as Dad joins her side, and I can't help but return their smiles as he utters those heart stopping words.

"No, Fruit Loop, you're perfect."

Epilogue – Christmas Eve, Eve, Eve - 1 Year Later

- Brimley Dawson

"I swear to God, wifey, if this is last year all over again, I'm divorcing you and then going to go to jail for a very, very long time!" Shaun shouts as we sprint through the airport.

I laugh. "Why you going to jail?" I shout at his back as he runs in front of me.

"Murder," he shouts over his shoulder, and I crack up, stopping to bend over, holding my sides as my cheeks start to hurt from laughing so much.

"No, no, I can't sleep without a light on after that night. We are getting on that plane, honey I will not be heading back to the Saltwood motel this year." He comes up to me, smiling and pulling at my arm and dragging me towards our terminal.

"I think you're more Grinchy this year than last," I say, panting between words as we stop at the desk to get our boarding passes checked.

"Bullshit! How so? We are getting on this plane, there is no snow to redirect us— we are nowhere near the position we were in last year!" he cries out.

A throat clears. "Mr and Mrs Dawson." The lady we handed our passes and passports to calls for our attention; she smiles weakly at us both and I start to laugh again, knowing exactly what's about to come out her mouth. If Shaun was a cartoon character right now, he'd have steam bellowing out of his ears.

"I'm afraid we've already done the last call for this flight, but if you head over to that desk in the corner," she pauses to point, "we might be able to get you on the next flight back to New York City, but don't hold me to it." She adds a finishing touch of a wink at Shaun.

I turn with sloth- like speed and a huge toothy grin on show and face him. I chuckle. "Well, hubby, I guess we are about to find out if you are more Grinch like this year after all." I wink with one eye and then the other. He gapes at me, his mouth in a perfect O shape, and shakes his head from side to side before pulling me into him and kissing me passionately, sucking the air from my lungs.

"You've done this on purpose, haven't you, Fruit Loop?"

The End.

Afterword

Hello my lovelies,

Thank you so much for reading my little christmas novella, i do hope you loved my Brimley and Shaun. This novella was such a stress-free one to write for me. I have always loved christmas, and road trip romances so combining the two was so much fun to do.

I want to give a quick thank you to all of my readers, friends and family for taking the time to support me on this crazy journey. You have no idea how much your kind words and love keeps me going.

So, until the next time. I hope you all have a wonderful christmas and a very happy new year.

Yours merrily,
Laura
xoxo

About The Author

Laura Rush

 Laura Rush is 30 years old, releasing her debut novel Yours Truly June 2023!

She lives In North Yorkshire, UK with her husband, son and dog.

Laura writes Rom com romances with a hella load of smut.

She enjoys martinis, long walks and reading.

Find her on socials

Instagram - @authorlaurarush

Facebook - @authorlaurarush

TikTok - @authorlaurarush

Website and newsletter coming soon!